Sweet Magnolia

by Virginia Kroll
illustrated by Laura Jacques

For Nancy, my sister, with love – V.K.

Library of Congress Cataloging-in-Publication-Data
Kroll, Virginia L.
Sweet magnolia / by Virginia Kroll; illustrated by Laura Jacques.
        p.   cm.
Summary: Denise visits her grandmother, a wildlife rehabilitator, in the Louisiana bayou and helps heal and free an injured baby bird.
    ISBN 0-88106-415-7 (reinforced for library use)
    ISBN 0-88106-414-9 (softcover)
    [1. Wildlife rescue—Fiction. 2. Bayous—Fiction. 3. Louisiana-Fiction.] I. Jacques, Laura, ill. II. Title.
PZ7.K9227Sw   1995
[E]—dc20

                                            93-11966
                                                CIP
                                                 AC

Published by Charlesbridge Publishing
85 Main Street, Watertown, MA 02472
(617) 926-0329
www.charlesbridge.com

Printed in South Korea
(hc) 10   9   8   7   6   5   4   3
(sc) 10   9   8   7

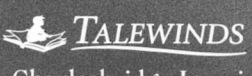

TALEWINDS
A Charlesbridge Imprint

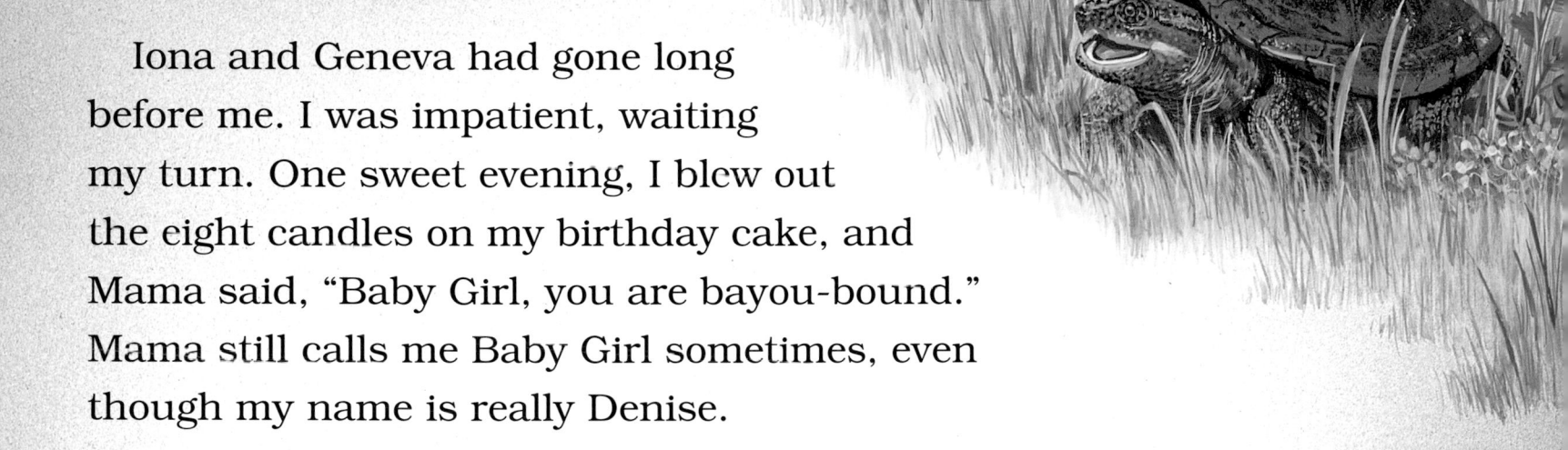

Iona and Geneva had gone long
before me. I was impatient, waiting
my turn. One sweet evening, I blew out
the eight candles on my birthday cake, and
Mama said, "Baby Girl, you are bayou-bound."
Mama still calls me Baby Girl sometimes, even
though my name is really Denise.

The bayou is where my Grandma lives, a place
swamped in mystery to me. Now, I'd get to see it for
myself. "What's it like in the bayou?" I asked, just to
give myself a head start.

Iona answered in a Halloween voice, "You'll be
knee-deep in marsh reed with alligators snapping at
your ankles and mosquitoes buzzing so loud in your
ears, you won't be able to hear the bullfrogs croak.
And those giant snapping turtles—ooh whee!"

"Stop that talk," Mama scolded as my eyes pleaded. "The bayou is full of creatures living in peace together and wonderful treasures to find."

"Sure is," Geneva agreed. "It's also a foot-stomping, cricket-chirping, music-playing, hand-clapping, happy place."

"Yes," said Mama, looking dreamy. "Folks there have *joie de vivre.*"

I frowned and Geneva explained. "That's a Cajun expression for *joy of life*, and wait till you hear them play the *zydeco* music!"

"Liveliest music there is," Iona broke in. She started clapping her hands and singing harmony to a tune in her head.

I decided to make up my own mind about the bayou.

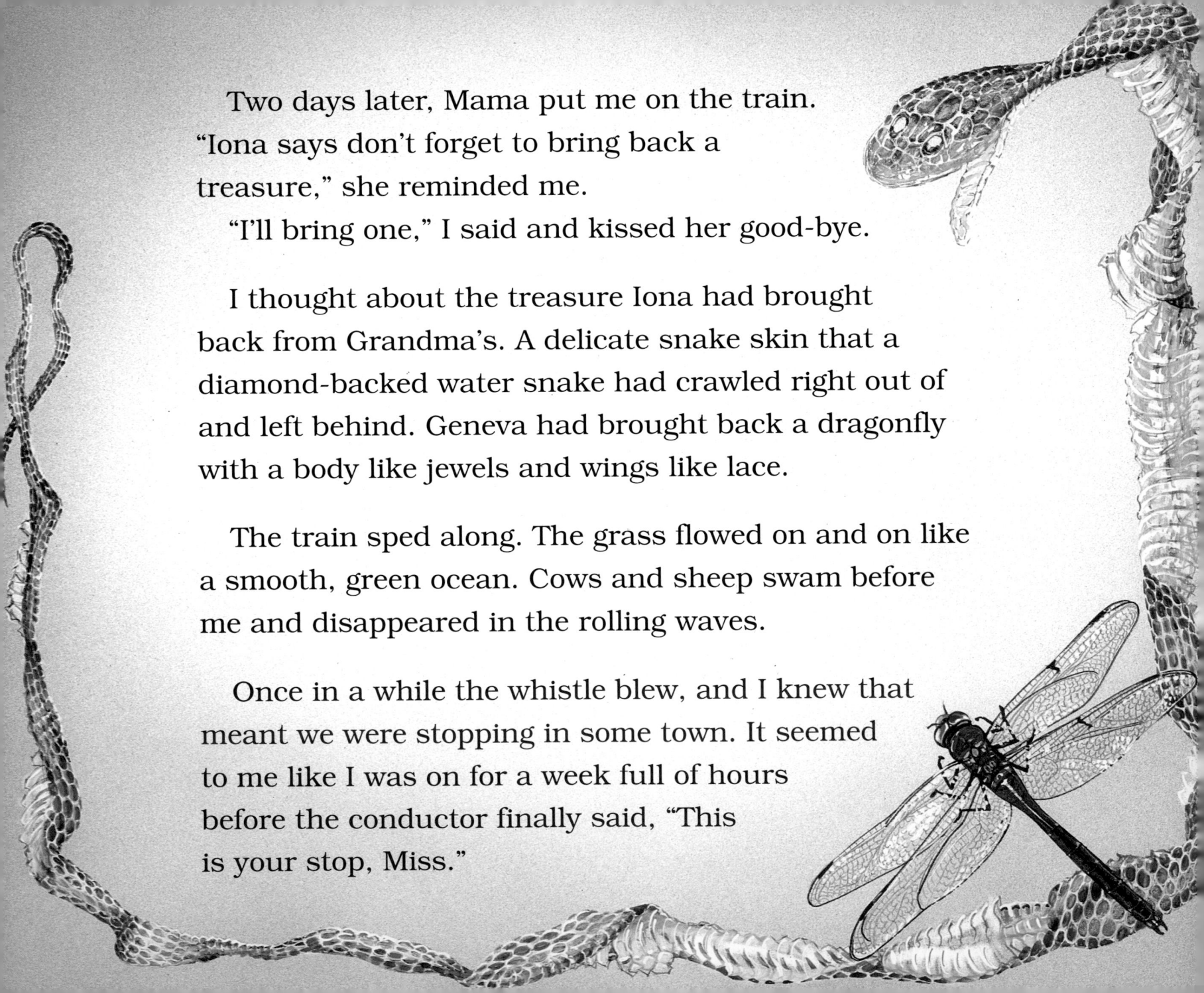

Two days later, Mama put me on the train.
"Iona says don't forget to bring back a
treasure," she reminded me.

"I'll bring one," I said and kissed her good-bye.

I thought about the treasure Iona had brought
back from Grandma's. A delicate snake skin that a
diamond-backed water snake had crawled right out of
and left behind. Geneva had brought back a dragonfly
with a body like jewels and wings like lace.

The train sped along. The grass flowed on and on like
a smooth, green ocean. Cows and sheep swam before
me and disappeared in the rolling waves.

Once in a while the whistle blew, and I knew that
meant we were stopping in some town. It seemed
to me like I was on for a week full of hours
before the conductor finally said, "This
is your stop, Miss."

My suitcase and I got off and stood waiting. Suddenly Grandma was standing there, smiling at me. "My, my, my!" she exclaimed. Her eyes said even more than her words.

We got into her truck. She flicked on the radio, and I heard some lively music. "Is that 'Zydeco Gris Gris' by Beausoleil?" I asked.

"Why, Denise, how did you know that?" Grandma asked. "That's such a big mouthful coming from such a little mouth."

I laughed and started clapping just like Iona.

Buds were exploding into leaves. Flowers decorated the roadsides. "Where I live, all the trees and flowers are still sleeping," I told her.

"Yeah," said Grandma. "Further south you come, the earlier things wake up." She drove up to her house.

"Grandma! Why is your house up on posts?"

"Well," Grandma laughed. "If you had been here just a few weeks ago, you'd think you were on an island, the way the water rises this time of year. One step out my door, and you'd be afloat."

I pictured myself and Grandma lying on our backs and paddling with our hands through the water, easy as you please.

"Where's the bayou?" I asked. I couldn't wait to see it.

Grandma pointed. "Down beyond. We'll go tomorrow. You don't want to go into the bayou at night. The mosquitoes are out."

"I know," I said. "They buzz so loud, you can't even hear the bullfrogs croak."

Grandma threw back her head with a hearty HAH. "Sounds just like Iona. I thought she stayed at home this time," she chuckled.

The way it got dark was as if a big, black curtain were being drawn all of a sudden. The air grew cold and snaked in where it could.

Grandma and I ate a soup called *gumbo*. "Yum! What's in this, Grandma?" I asked between slurps.

"Okra, for one thing. Some crawfish, some rice, onions, and my special spices," she said.

I was asleep before Grandma finished reading me a story.

In the morning, I thought I was still dreaming because the first thing I saw was a deer peeking in the window. Grandma laughed at my wide-eyed look.

"Looks like he wants to come in," I said.

"He does," she answered, pouring cereal for us.

"Then why don't you let him?"

"Uh uh," Grandma said. "Wouldn't be fair. Wild critters need to find their own food. Oh, I fed him when he was hurt, but now he's on his own. He just has to get used to being a deer."

We ate our cereal and I asked Grandma, "How long have you been a *wildlife rehabilitator*?"

"My, my! You sure do have a way with big, important words!" she said. I felt proud that I had remembered the name of her job.

"I got my license about ten years ago, but I've been helping critters long as I can recall."

"Can I see your other critters, Grandma?"

We went outside. A screech owl blinked at us from one cage. In another, a bobcat with a bandaged foot was eating, and a fox with a stitched-up side was watching us.

Grandma introduced me. "Winkin' Owl, Hunter Bobcat, and Tippy Fox, this is my granddaughter Denise." She filled a bottle and handed it to me. Tippy began to yelp.

"Wow! You mean I get to feed him?" "That's right," Grandma said. Tippy closed his hungry mouth around the nipple and drank it dry in two minutes flat.

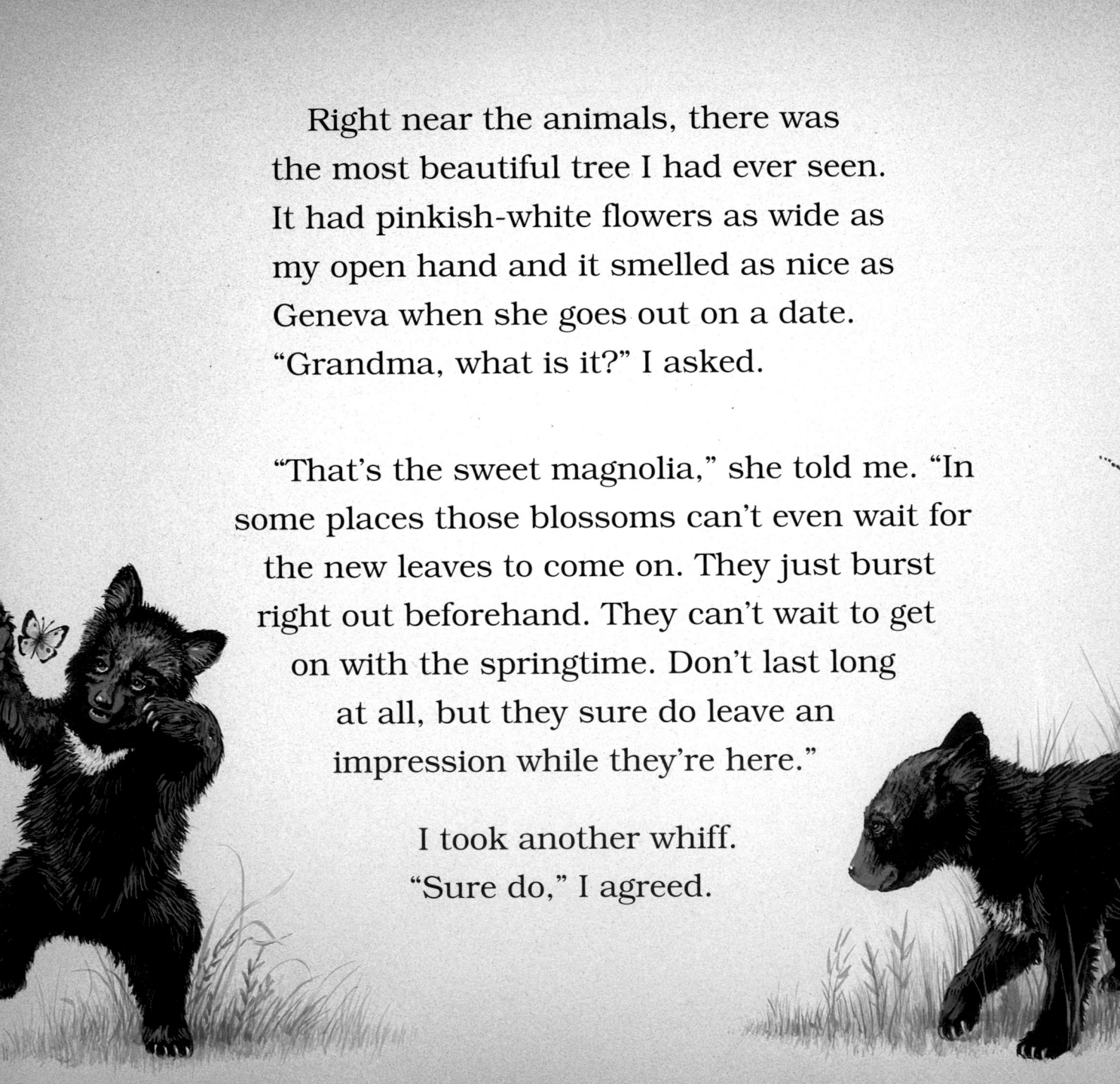

Right near the animals, there was
the most beautiful tree I had ever seen.
It had pinkish-white flowers as wide as
my open hand and it smelled as nice as
Geneva when she goes out on a date.
"Grandma, what is it?" I asked.

"That's the sweet magnolia," she told me. "In
some places those blossoms can't even wait for
the new leaves to come on. They just burst
right out beforehand. They can't wait to get
on with the springtime. Don't last long
at all, but they sure do leave an
impression while they're here."

I took another whiff.
"Sure do," I agreed.

"Let's go see the bayou," said Grandma.

We got into Grandma's boat. Soon we came to a different-sounding place. We got out of the boat, and I hushed so I could hear it all—tiny tickings, gentle jigglings, ripplings, and rustlings—little life sounds all around.

"Talk about trees!" I gasped, looking up. They were hunched over like bent giants. Moss was hanging in shaggy clumps from their branches like ragged curtains. "The bayou," I whispered.

Suddenly I heard a tiny cheeping. There was some pain and fear in it. "Over there," said Grandma, pointing.

I ran, then stopped short, pitching backwards like a cartoon character so I wouldn't step on the struggling bird.

Grandma carefully scooped it up. She shook her head.

"Can you fix it, Grandma?"

Grandma warned me, "Sometimes nature doesn't see things our way." But she looked in my eyes, and we took the bird on home.

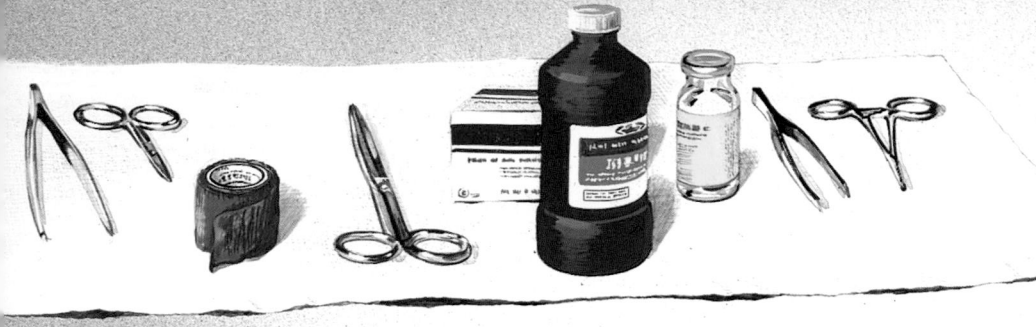

"What happened to it, Grandma?" I asked.

Grandma examined the panting bird. "Hmm. Broken leg. I reckon she was too impatient, Denise. Burst right out of her nest ahead of schedule. Couldn't wait to get on with the springtime."

"She's just too full of *joie de vivre*," I said.

"Indeed!" Grandma said. She shook her head and smiled, and I knew I had surprised her with my big words again.

She fed the bird with a tiny tube, then set the broken leg and taped it. I studied the soft feathers and fluffy markings.

"What kind is she?" I asked.

"A painted bunting," Grandma said.

Grandma kept up the feedings day and night. I helped. The painted bunting grew bigger and more colorful and got its flight feathers. Pretty soon she was pecking seeds right out of my hand.

"Don't feed her from your hand all the time," Grandma said, "or she won't learn how to find seeds and insects on her own."

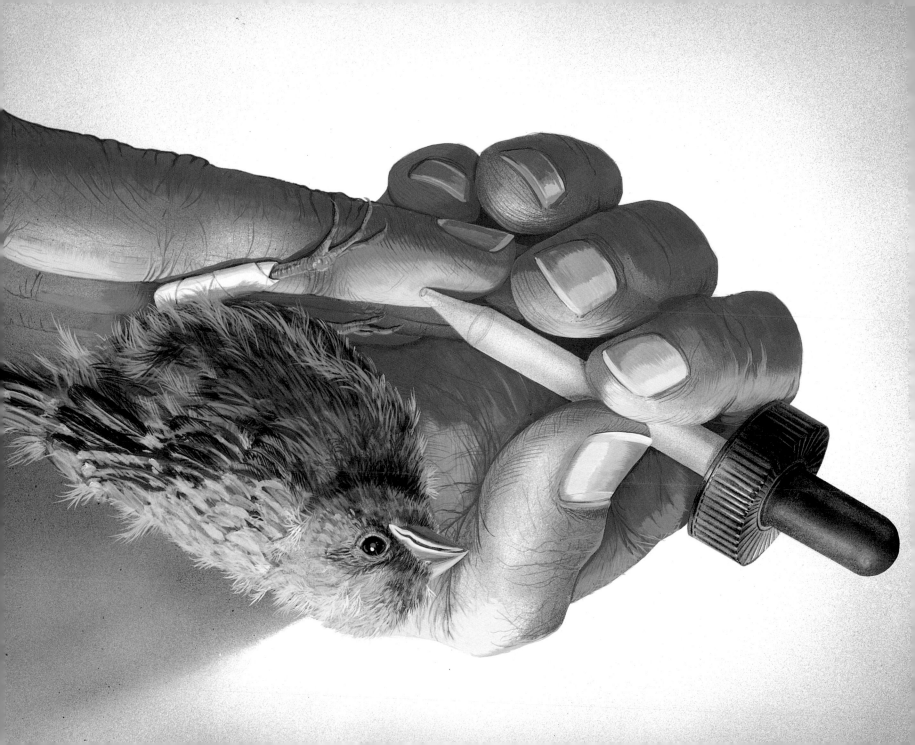

The day Grandma unwrapped the bunting's leg, she asked, "You gonna give this one a name? She's yours. You found her, after all."

My heart skipped like a stone across a stream. Mine! Did Grandma mean it? Wait till Iona and Geneva saw the treasure I was bringing home!

I looked at my bird. I thought about how she tried to fly too soon and how Grandma said she was impatient, just like the sweet magnolia flowers.

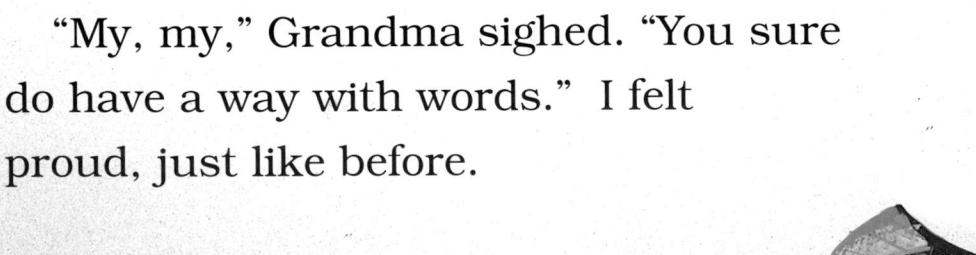

"Sweet Magnolia!" I said. "That's her name."

"My, my," Grandma sighed. "You sure do have a way with words." I felt proud, just like before.

One morning after breakfast, Grandma said,
"This is the big day. Come on."

I followed, wondering what was so special. She went to
Sweet Magnolia's cage and opened the door. Then she stopped.
"You ought to do it, Denise. You found her, after all."

"Do what, Grandma?" I asked.

"Set her flying to the winds," she answered.

I tried staring some sense into Grandma. She nodded toward the cage.

"You mean let her go?" I squeaked.

"Of course," Grandma began.

"But Grandma, she's MINE!" I shouted. "You even
said so. She's the treasure I'm taking home."

Grandma half-smiled, half-frowned. "I'm sorry,
Denise. Maybe I didn't explain it right and you
misunderstood. She's yours to help . . . yours to
heal . . . yours to set free."

I put my hands on my hips and stamped
my foot. "No."

"You love her, don't you?" Grandma said.

I thought for a moment. I gulped.
I blinked hard. I opened the cage and
slowly put my hand in.

Sweet Magnolia jumped onto my finger. She clung to me with her little claws as if she didn't want to let me go either. We boated to the bayou and walked to the tree where we had first found her. She flapped her wings once but stayed perched on my hand.

We stood listening to the little life sounds. Sweet Magnolia tipped her head as if she heard something. Then she flapped her wings and flew to a branch just an arm's length away.

She looked at me and didn't move.

"See, Grandma? She wants to stay."

Grandma cupped a hand over my shoulder. A second passed. Sweet Magnolia said CHEE-UP and took off over the trees where I couldn't see her. "We'd better wait, just in case she comes back," I said.

Grandma cooperated for a long time. Then we started back to her house.

"Don't feel bad, Denise. We'll find you another *lagniappe*."

"What's a lan-yap?" I asked.

"It's Cajun for a special bonus— something like a gift you get for just being you."

After lunch, Grandma told me
to take a rest. "We are going to
a *fais dodo* tonight."

"What's a fay doh doh?" I asked.

"A party, child," she said, "with singing
and dancing and lots of *jambalaya*."

"Yum," I said, remembering Grandma's
spicy shrimp stew.

"Will they play *zydeco*, Grandma?"

"Yes, indeed!"

And Grandma was right. It was great! There were lots of people
enjoying each other's music and each other's food. After a long
time they put me to bed along with all the other kids.

"How do you feel now?" Grandma asked, as she tucked me in.

I thought for a couple seconds. "Full of *joie de vivre*,"
I said. And the joy of life was still inside me when she
took me back to her house the next morning.

During the next few days, I saw a purple
gallinule family, looking like chickens hopping
over lily pads. I saw fireflies as big as nickels and
a water rat with a tail as long as my arm!

The day before my visit was over, Grandma and I spotted
a huge, old alligator looking like a stiff, fallen log sunning its bumpy
body. At dusk, we got out of the bayou before the mosquitoes started
humming, and we listened to the bullfrogs croaking
from the comfort of Grandma's house.

On my last day, I said good-bye to Grandma's creatures.
"Winkin' will be leaving next," she said. I walked over to the
smallest cage, the one where we had kept my
painted bunting. I sighed a lonely sigh.
Then I saw something. I reached in and took
it and held it against my cheek. I showed it to
Grandma and told her it was my lan-yap.

Grandma put me and my suitcase into her truck. I traveled back on the train. It seemed like days till the conductor said it was my stop.

Mama squeezed me tight and called me Baby Girl as always.

Iona and Geneva were happy to see me, too. Right away they asked, "What'd you bring back? Come on, let's see."

"A lan-yap," I answered.

They looked at me as if I were crazy. I smiled. "A Sweet Magnolia feather. Tell you about it later."

First I needed to take my treasure out to look at it alone and put it in a safe, forever place.